Searching
the
Lights

Searching the Lights

~ ~ ~

story by **Margie Willis Clary**

illustrations by Valerie Jeanne Luedtke

SANDLAPPER PUBLISHING CO., INC.
ORANGEBURG, SOUTH CAROLINA

Copyright © 1998 by Margie Willis Clary

First Edition

Published by Sandlapper Publishing Co., Inc.
Orangeburg, South Carolina

Printed in Korea

Library of Congress Cataloging-in-Publication Data

Clary, Margie Willis, 1931–
    Searching the lights / by Margie Willis Clary ; illustrations by
Valerie Luedtke.
       p.   cm.
    Summary: With the help of his grandfather, Jim researches his
favorite lighthouse for a school project and in the process learns
about the father he lost to the Gulf War. Includes brief histories
of the lighthouses of South Carolina.
    ISBN 0-87844-138-7
    [1. Fathers and sons—Fiction. 2. Grandfathers—Fiction.
3. Lighthouses—Fiction. 4. South Carolina—Fiction.]   I. Luedtke,
Valerie, 1954–   ill.   II. Title.
PZ7.C5627Se   1998
[E]—dc21   97-39641
                                             CIP
                                             AC

Dedicated to . . .

my family
Ralph, Wayne, Debbie, Sheila, and Grady
Caleb, Jill, and Scott

A special dedication to . . .

the preservationists
of the Morris Island Lighthouse
Charleston, South Carolina

Special thanks to . . .

my nephews
Hampton Young of Mount Pleasant, South Carolina,
who served as the model for Jim
and Michael Willis of Laurens, South Carolina,
who provided some of the lighthouse photographs

—Margie Willis Clary

and

Special thanks to . . .

Robert Gillgrist
who served as the model for Grandpa

—Valerie Jeanne Luedtke

Searching
the
Lights

"THANKS, MRS. BAILEY. SEE YOU TOMORROW. I'll call you later tonight, Drew," Jim said as he stepped from the car and slammed the door.

He waved to the Baileys and then scuffed toward the front steps of his Oak Island home near Charleston, South Carolina. He unlocked the front door and let himself in. As he walked through the hallway into the kitchen, he grumbled, "If only I didn't have to study." He threw his bookbag on a kitchen stool and opened the refrigerator. Taking out a carton of juice, he poured himself a glass and began drinking as he turned to look out the kitchen window.

Down below, at the edge of the yard, Grandpa was fishing from the family's dock. Beyond the dock lay the marsh. The saltwater marsh grass looked golden in the sunlight. It was high tide, and the waters of Folly River filled the marshland. Out past the marsh was Morris Island, and Jim's eyes rested on the towering image of the island lighthouse. The tower's red and white stripes made it seem nearer than it really was. For as long as he could remember, Jim and his family had called the Morris Island lighthouse *"our* lighthouse."

To Jim, this view was awesome. It always reminded him of his dad. Seeing the lighthouse made him feel lonely, yet at the same time it gave him a feeling of security. A blurry memory flashed before his eyes whenever he looked at the lighthouse. Even after seven years, he still could not figure out where this memory came from.

Jim and his mom had moved in with Grandpa when his dad did not return from the Gulf War. Jim had the same mixed feelings of loneliness and security each time he and Grandpa made a visit to the Morris Island lighthouse.

Jim's heart leaped as he thought of climbing the old lighthouse steps—*all 201 of them*. What an adventure! Before long, the weather would be warm enough for them to make another visit.

Mom always worried about those adventures. Before Grandpa and Jim could leave the house, she would give them her usual lecture about the dangers of the rotting pilings and the rusting latticed staircase. Grandpa would nod his head and say, "I'll be careful and take good care of *our* boy." Then he'd give Jim an appeasing wink.

Grandpa and Jim always visited the lighthouse at low tide when its base was completely surrounded by the sandbar. Sometimes they walked from Folly Beach to the foot of the lighthouse. Other times they went by boat.

The difficult part of the adventure was the climb to the entrance across the broken concrete and the rough barnacles that clung to the foundation. Jim thought it scary that erosion was slowly eating away at the foundation. He always felt relieved when he was finally inside the lighthouse and had begun to ascend the circular staircase. He knew that when he reached the top, the effort would have been worthwhile.

In spite of the dangers they faced, Jim and Grandpa always mastered the climb.

The young adventurer smiled to himself. "Grandpa surely won't go to the lighthouse on a weekend and fight the boat traffic," he thought. "That's the time the sandbar is invaded by fishermen, shell seekers, and history buffs. We'll probably go during spring break."

Jim's thoughts were interrupted by the bark of his dog Rex. This was a sign that fishing was good. Looking down toward the dock, he could see a large fish dangling from the end of Grandpa's line.

"Man, if only I could be there fishing with Grandpa," he said. "Seems as if Ms. Wheeler could have given us some slack about the assignment for the weekend."

It was true that he had known about the history project for two weeks but, like most of the class, he had put it off. By Monday morning he must hand in a topic with a prepared outline. This would mean going to the library on Saturday and probably again on Sunday. "Mom's not going to like all those trips into town," he muttered to himself.

If only he could come up with a subject to write about.

Jim turned from the window and sat down at the kitchen table. He removed the lid from the cookie jar, took out two cookies, then replaced the lid. As he sat munching, he ran his fingers over the painted scene on the jar. It was a scene of a lighthouse. Ever since he was small, Jim had thought the painting on the cookie jar was of *his* lighthouse. He looked closely, trying to make out the name of the artist, but it was too tiny. . . . *Yes, the picture was interesting, but it wasn't getting his assignment started. . . .*

Jim finished the cookies and juice, then picked up his bookbag.

As he dragged out the history book, he heard Rex's bark just outside the house and Grandpa's footsteps on the deck. The back door swung open and in walked Grandpa, with Rex at his heels. Grandpa was carrying a bucket. In it were several nice-sized saltwater bass.

Rex rushed toward the table and jumped. His front paws landed on Jim's lap as he gave his master's face a quick lick.

"Hey, boy!" Jim said, giving Rex's head a hard rubbing. "How ya doin'?"

"Hi, son," Grandpa said as he placed the cleaned fish on the counter. "I thought it was time for you to be home. Why didn't you come join me?"

"Couldn't, Grandpa. I've got studying to do."

"You always have to study. What's so special about today?"

"I've got to choose a topic and come up with an outline for a history project by Monday morning." Jim groaned.

"Did you just find this out today?"

Jim hung his head, a little embarrassed. "Well, I've known about the assignment for two weeks. I just haven't given it much thought."

"Best get to thinking then," said Grandpa as he sat down on the other side of the table facing Jim.

"If only I could think of a topic," Jim lamented, "then maybe I'd know where to begin."

"That *would* help," agreed Grandpa. "You know, finding a topic shouldn't be such a problem since you're living in the lap of history. Much of the Civil War was fought right here on these waters—the Battle of Fort Wagner, the Battle of Secessionville, Fort Sumter—"

Jim jumped to his feet and shouted, "I don't want to read or write about war!"

Grandpa quickly responded, "I'm sorry, son. I just wanted to help. Yes, we do know the terrible woes of war. Maybe it's still too soon for you to get into war research, but it is an important part of history and the war fought here happened a long time ago. Why not write about your great-great-great-grandfather being stationed on James Island during the Civil War? His letters will give you plenty of information for a research paper."

Jim slowly sat back down. "I guess I could, but that's still about war. I really want to write about something I know about."

As he said these words, the mixed emotions he always felt when he looked at *their* lighthouse rushed through him, and that vague memory of his dad returned.

Almost yelling, Jim said excitedly, "Grandpa, I want to write about the Morris Island lighthouse—*our* lighthouse. There's so much you've told me about the place, and we've made so many memories on its sandbar. It will be a great topic for a research paper!"

Grandpa was thrilled about Jim's topic choice. "It surely will be," he said. "Your mom and I both can give you information, but you'll have to go to the library to find the history of the lighthouse. Your computer will be another help. You should be able to find out the current status of the lighthouse on the Internet."

Grandpa stopped talking and sat silent for a minute. Rubbing his chin, he looked directly at Jim. In a soft voice, he began, "You know, your dad was one of the biggest lighthouse buffs of his generation. Before he left for the Gulf, he had plans to take you and your mom to the Outer Banks of North Carolina to see the lighthouses there. When he did not return from the war, your mom lost interest in lighthouses. I'm glad to see an interest being renewed. It's about time."

Grandpa paused. Rising quietly to his feet, he turned and walked out of the room.

Jim took little notice of Grandpa's movements. He sat staring into space absorbing what he had just heard about his dad and the lighthouse. That vague memory flashed again in his mind. This time he could make out part of his dad's face and a sandbar. . . . *If only he could remember* . . . .

The vision faded as he heard Grandpa moving things around in the storage room downstairs. Then a door slammed.

Grandpa returned to the kitchen carrying a large book.

"What's that?" Jim asked.

"Something that belonged to your father," answered Grandpa. He dusted the book off with a dishcloth and placed it on the table.

It was a scrapbook—an overly stuffed scrapbook.

Opening the book to the first page, Grandpa said, "This should help you with your assignment."

Jim was speechless. The scrapbook was filled with pictures, newspaper clippings, brochures, and other mementos about lighthouses—the lighthouses of South Carolina.

LIGHTHOUSES - S.C. HISTORY

[illegible]

Hilton Head Lighthouse
1891

Harbour Town Lighthouse - 1969

Hunting Island Lighthouse
3rd grade class trip

THE NEWEST   IN S.C.

"Wow and double wow!" exclaimed Jim. "Will it ever! I can't believe you've never told me about Dad's interest in lighthouses. I thought he just liked *our* lighthouse."

"He liked the whole subject of lighthouses," replied Grandpa. "Why, he even bought this cookie jar for your mom while they were honeymooning in Massachusetts. He thought the lighthouse in the painting looked like the Morris Island lighthouse."

Grandpa sat down beside Jim and pointed to a picture in the scrapbook. "This is the Hunting Island lighthouse, near Beaufort. That's where your dad's interest in lighthouses began. When he was in the third grade and studying South Carolina history, his class went to Hunting Island on a field trip. He was so fascinated by the lighthouse he climbed its staircase three times that day. Here's a picture of his class taken on the steps of the lighthouse. That's your dad, the one looking up at the tower."

"Say, he looks like me!" exclaimed Jim.

"*You look like him* would be more like it," Grandpa replied.

"What else happened that day?" asked Jim.

"I don't know what else happened *that* day," Grandpa answered, "but after that trip your dad read everything he could find about lighthouses. He wrote to several park rangers and to the United States Lighthouse Service for information. That's where some of these brochures came from.

"In 1969, we went on vacation to Hilton Head Island and visited the lighthouse at Palmetto Dunes. We had to get permission to go there since the old tower stands on the golf course at the private resort. It's known as the Leamington light, built in 1891. It is said to be haunted by the 'Lady in Blue.' That's the legend told of the Adam Fripp family after the hurricane of 1898.

"Read on. I'm sure your dad had a copy of the legend someplace. It's good reading.

"We also visited the lighthouse at Harbour Town on the Sea Pines Plantation. It was brand new. We climbed its steps several times. We went once after dark to see the flashing lights. Although it's not recognized as an *official* lighthouse, to your dad it was a *real* lighthouse, beacon and all."

Grandpa turned a page of the scrapbook and pointed to a picture of a house with a tower built in the roof. "This is the lighthouse at Haig Point on Daufuskie Island," he said.

"That's a funny looking lighthouse!" exclaimed Jim.

"It's different all right," Grandpa responded. "It was built in 1873. The beacon was mounted on the keeper's house. In 1883, a second lighthouse was built on the island, on Bloody Point Plantation. Its beacon was also mounted on the keeper's house. Both lighthouses had range lights to help guide ships into the Savannah River. The lights were used until 1924. The houses are still standing, but the light has been removed from the top of the one at Bloody Point. I've seen them both. They *are* interesting— kind of *quaint*."

"Quaint?" asked Jim. "I suppose they are unusual. I'd like to see them."

"I wouldn't mind visiting them again myself," said Grandpa. "We'll try to go there during the summer. You'd get to ride on the ferryboat that runs from Hilton Head to Daufuskie—by boat is the only way to get onto the island."

"That will be a fun trip. I can't wait," Jim replied.

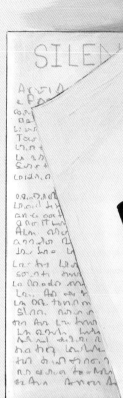

SILEN

Morris Island Lighthouse
1988

Haig Point - Daufuskie Island - 1873

Years of Erosion
Morris Island

The front door opened and in walked Jim's mother, from work.

"What are my guys doing?" she asked as she reached the kitchen.

"We are *searching the lights*, Mom, *searching the lights*."

She managed to smile as she noticed the scrapbook. "Your dad would be happy to know his book has come to life again," she said. "He would want you to research the lights."

She patted Jim on the shoulder and turned away to hide the tears in her eyes. Quickly changing the subject, she said, "Thanks, Grandpa. I see we have fresh fish for dinner."

"You're very welcome," replied Grandpa, as he turned a page of the scrapbook.

"Hey!" exclaimed Jim. "This page is all about *our* lighthouse here on Morris Island. Look at all these old pictures. Some are taken from the sandbar and others from the top of the tower. Here's one that shows the broken concrete of the foundation. Man, this is cool! Who took all these pictures?"

"I took some of them, but your dad took most," Grandpa replied. "He was a real 'shutterbug' when it came to the Morris Island lighthouse."

"There's so much material here on the Morris Island light. It'll take me a whole day to read it all!" Jim proclaimed.

"You've got all weekend," said Grandpa, "and you can make your outline while you're reading."

"Good idea. That's the way to go," Jim replied.

Jim flipped through the many pages concerning the Morris Island tower and stopped at the next lighthouse, the one on Sullivan's Island. He knew this was the one that took over the work of the Morris Island light in 1962. Jim had visited there many times.

"I don't think this tower looks like a lighthouse," he said. "It's too modern looking."

"It doesn't offer the same mystery that the older towers do," said Grandpa. "The old towers have withstood decades of hurricanes and storms. That attracts people to them. They're a real part of history. We just have to accept that the role of the old beacons has been taken over by modern technology."

"I guess so," said Jim, "but I still like the old towers best. There's something *good* about them. Just think of all the lives they've saved over the years. The modern ones won't ever give me the same feelings the older ones do."

"Those were your dad's sentiments exactly," said Grandpa. "He liked the historical ones too."

The next page was dedicated to the lighthouses on Cape Romain, near McClellanville.

"There are two lighthouses there," Grandpa said, "a tall black and white one, which leans slightly, and a short one made of brick. The brick one is the oldest *original* lighthouse in Charleston County. I went there once with my fishing buddy Fred.

"You know, Fred was born at Cape Romain. His father was lighthouse keeper there for several years. When your dad was about your age, Fred and I would take him fishing with us. Fred told him all sorts of ghost tales about the old lighthouses. The tales are said to be true."

"I'd sure like to hear them," said Jim. "Do you think he'd come fishing with us sometimes?"

"I'm sure he'd be glad to come," Grandpa answered. "I'll call him next week and invite him."

"Yes! Yes! I can't wait!" cried Jim.

"Hey, fellows," Jim's mom called from the other side of the kitchen, "I hate to break up the *search of the lights*, but dinner is ready. You're going to have to move the book so I can set the table. Jim, why not take it on up to your room and wash up for dinner."

"Just a minute longer, O.K? We only have one page to go," Jim said as he turned to the last page of the scrapbook.

"This is the North Island lighthouse," Grandpa told him. "It stands at the entrance to Winyah Bay in Georgetown County. Your dad went to school with an Ellis boy whose grandfather was the lighthouse keeper. He told your dad there were many mysterious happenings in that old lighthouse."

"It must be true," said Jim. "Look, here's a newspaper clipping that reads, 'Lighthouse has Unknown Visitors.' I'd like to visit there too. In fact, I'd like to visit all the lighthouses in South Carolina."

"I hope you can, son. I hope you can," replied Grandpa. "Now, take the scrapbook up to your room. You can do more research after dinner."

Jim replaced the clipping and carefully closed the cover. Then he rose from his chair.

As he lifted the heavy scrapbook, a photograph fell from its pages onto the table.

Jim gasped. The picture was the image that always flashed before his eyes when he looked at the Morris Island light! It was a picture of his dad standing on a sandbar, holding a small boy in his arms. In the background was *their* lighthouse.

"That's it!" Jim shouted. "Now I see it all. I see his face—and that's me and *our* lighthouse!"

"What's the excitement all about, son?" Grandpa asked, picking up the photo.

"That's the picture in my mind—the one I've been trying to remember," said Jim. "When and where was it taken?"

Grandpa moved his fingers slowly over the photograph as if caressing a treasure. He looked puzzled as he answered, "I took that picture of you and your dad on the sandbar in front of *our* lighthouse just two months before the Gulf War. I have a copy, but I don't understand how this one got here."

Jim's mother wiped her hands on a towel and walked over to the table. She took the picture from Grandpa's hand and calmly said, "This is my copy. I put it in the scrapbook. I wanted Jim to have it someday. It's one of our family's last memories."

A hush filled the room as the three stared at the photograph.

Jim put his arms around his mom and hugged her tightly. Then, without a word, he moved toward the window and looked across the marsh, fixing his gaze on the lighthouse. He suddenly felt very safe. That feeling of loneliness was all gone. The memory was no longer a blur. He remembered everything. Best of all, he could see his father's face.

As Jim crossed the kitchen, heading for the stairs, he called to Grandpa, "I thought this research paper was going to be a real pain, but it's turning out to be great. Not only am I *searching the lights*, but I'm discovering awesome memories of my dad."

The Lighthouse

The lighthouse stands alone
Looking out onto the sea.
It's stood for years so tall
For all the world to see.
It's heard the ship's far call
And led the sailors home.
Its silhouette against the sky
Gave a peaceful calm.

Its beacon no longer is aglow,
Its lens and lantern gone.
There's no one there to walk the stairs
Or watch the barnacles grow.
Graffiti is now upon its walls
Some bricks are breaking fast.
But to the lovers of the sea,
Tis a mystic symbol of the past.

—Margie W. Clary
© 1997

Brief Histories of
THE LIGHTHOUSES OF SOUTH CAROLINA

CAPE ROMAIN

There are two lighthouses on Lighthouse Island at Cape Romain, near the town of McClellanville.

The first, a sixty-five-foot red-brick tower, was built in 1827 eighty-seven feet above sea level. It is the oldest of its kind still standing in the United States. The lighthouse was found to be too short for good service and was replaced in 1857. Its beacon was removed for use in the new tower. Today the brick structure resembles a large smokestack.

The 1857 lighthouse, a 150-foot octagonal-shaped tower, has 195 steps leading to the top. The lantern room and lens were destroyed by Confederate troops in 1861, but the light was back in service in 1866 and continued in use until 1947.

Both towers, freshly painted during the past five years, are part of the Cape Romain National Wildlife Refuge. They are not open to the public, but can be viewed by boat from the water.

Brad Nettles, POST AND COURIER

GEORGETOWN

The Georgetown lighthouse is located on North Island near the entrance to Winyah Bay. Built in the late 1790s, it is one of two lights that continue to shine on the South Carolina coast. The original wooden tower was destroyed by a hurricane in 1806 and replaced in 1812 by one of white-washed brick. Like most of the South Carolina lighthouses, the one at Georgetown was damaged during the Civil War. Rebuilt in 1867, the new tower stands eighty-five feet high and has 124 steps leading to the top. The lighthouse was in the direct path of Hurricane Hugo in 1989. The tower itself was not damaged but the light, now electrical, went out.

North Island is a beautiful unspoiled

Chip Smith

wildlife refuge, accessible only by boat. The majority of the island is owned by the state of South Carolina, with just a small portion allocated to the lighthouse. Because visitors are not allowed on the island, the lighthouse can be viewed only from the water.

This light is one of the few in the nation manned by the United States Coast Guard.

HAIG POINT

The Haig Point lighthouse was constructed in 1873 on Daufuskie Island, southwest of Hilton Head. The rear beacon was mounted in a small forty-foot tower on top of the keeper's house.

In 1883, a second light was built at the southeastern tip of Daufuskie Island. This one, known as the Bloody Point lighthouse, was also built on the keeper's two-story dwelling.

Both towers, which were used to guide ships into the Savannah River, operated until 1924. They were decommissioned in 1936. The two keepers' houses are still standing, but the tower has been removed from the Bloody Point light. The Haig Point lighthouse dwelling is now part of the Haig Point Resort community and is maintained by the International Paper Realty Corporation.

The Daufuskie Company

Daufuskie Island is accessible only by water. Vagabond Cruises run daily from Hilton Head Island. Visitors may also reach Daufuskie by taking a private boat from Beaufort or Bluffton.

HARBOUR TOWN

In 1969, a lighthouse was built on the southern tip of Hilton Head on Sea Pines Plantation. Constructed as part of a commemoration of the island's Heritage Golf Tournament, it was the first lighthouse since 1827 to be privately financed. The red and white tower is ninety-three feet high with 110 steps leading to the top. Although it is not recognized as an official lighthouse, the Harbour Town light serves as a private navigational aid for travelers on the Intracoastal Waterway. It is open to the public daily. A small admission fee must be paid to enter the gates to the private Sea Pines Plantation Resort.

Margie Clary

HILTON HEAD ISLAND

In 1863 a lighthouse was built on Leamington Plantation on Hilton Head Island. The original structure was destroyed by heavy winds in 1869 and was replaced in 1891. The cast-iron skeleton tower is ninety feet tall with 112 steps to the top. It operated as a beacon until the 1930s. Restored in 1986, it is said to be structurally intact and in good condition for its age.

Officially called the Hilton Head Lighthouse, the tower is often referred to as the Leamington Light. It is owned by the Greenwood Development Corporation and stands between the eighth and ninth greens of the golf course at Palmetto Dunes Resort. Guests at the resort may view the lighthouse, but it is open to the public only by special permission of the management group.

Yostie Ashley

HUNTING ISLAND

The first lighthouse built on Hunting Island, near Beaufort, was completed in 1859. Its use was short lived, as by 1862 it was reported to have fallen into the sea. Conflicting stories make it unclear whether it was destroyed by erosion or blown up by the Confederate army during the Civil War. In 1875 a new tower was constructed of interchangeable cast-iron sections so that it could be taken apart if necessary. Due to aggressive high tides and erosion, it was disassembled in 1889 and reassembled at its current site, a quarter mile south of the original tower. The new lighthouse was built upon an eight-inch concrete foundation. The top of the tower is 140 feet from the ground and is reached by 181 steps. The tower, 95 feet high, is lined with bricks. The oil-vapored light was used until its retirement in 1933.

The lighthouse is now a part of Hunting Island State Park and is open to the public daily for viewing and climbing.

Michael Willis

MORRIS ISLAND

The Morris Island lighthouse was the first to be erected in the southern states. Acting upon a decree from King George III, the tower was built at the southern entrance to Charleston Harbor in 1767. The original lighthouse was destroyed during the Civil War and a new tower built in 1876. The Morris Island light stands 161 feet high and has 201 steps leading to the top. It survived a major hurricane in 1885 and the great

Charleston earthquake in 1886. In 1938, the Coast Guard replaced the oil-vapored light with an automatic light. The beacon was extinguished in 1962 when its role was assumed by the new lighthouse on Sullivan's Island. The walls of the Morris Island lighthouse are believed to be structurally sound despite the beating from Hurricane Hugo in 1989.

Until recent years, the tower could be reached on foot at low tide from Folly Beach by crossing the sandbar on which the tower stands. Because of heavy erosion, this is no longer possible. The red-and-white-striped tower is visible from James Island and Folly Beach and can be viewed by boat from the harbor.

The Morris Island lighthouse is privately owned, but currently for sale. Its future is uncertain at this time.

Wayne Clary

SULLIVAN'S ISLAND

The Charleston area's youngest lighthouse was built in 1962 to replace the one on Morris Island. Unlike most lighthouses, the Charleston light, as it is known, was built of steel and has an elevator as well as stairs. The light mechanism has the potential of 28 million candlepower and is thereby capable of being one of the most powerful lights in the world. The Charleston light, which stands 163 feet high, was originally painted orange and white. The colors were not agreeable to the island residents, and the tower was repainted black and white. In 1982 the Charleston light was fully automated.

Located near historic Fort Moultrie, the Sullivan's Island lighthouse is manned by the United States Coast Guard. Access may be obtained through the Coast Guard office in Charleston.

Michael Willis

SELECTED BIBLIOGRAPHY

Anderson, Joe (park ranger, Caesars Head State Park—formerly at Hunting Island State Park). Interview by author. November 14, 1995.

Baldwin, William. "Carolina Lights," *South Carolina Wildlife* Magazine (March–April 1997): 15–2.

Burns, Billie. *An Island Named Daufuskie*. Daufuskie Island, SC: Billie Burn Books, 1991.

Griffin, Cassie. "The Lonely Towers," *South Carolina Wildlife* Magazine (January–February 1977): 27–41.

Hardin, Candace, and Kim McDermott. "The Passing of the Light," *The Charleston Magazine* (July–August 1989): 14–15, 52.

Hardin, Candace, and Kim McDermott. "Shining Beacons of the Coast," *The Charleston Magazine* (year-end 1991): 62–63.

Holland, Francis Ross, Jr. *America's Lighthouses, An Illustrated History*. New York: Dover Publications, Inc., 1972.

Kagerer, Rudy. *A Guidebook to Lighthouses in South Carolina, Georgia and Florida's East Coast*. Athens, GA: Lighthouses Enterprises, Inc., 1997.

McDermott, Kim. "Points of the Lights," *The Charleston Magazine*, (spring 1993): 32–38.

Rhyne, Nancy. *Touring the Coastal South Carolina Backroads*. Winston-Salem: John F. Blair, Publisher, 1992.

Roberts, Bruce, and Ray Jones. *Southern Lighthouses*, 2nd edition. Old Saybrook, CT: Globe Pequot Press, 1989.

Wichmann, Fred (Charleston realtor). Interview by author. October 29, 1995.

About the Author:

MARGIE WILLIS CLARY is a teacher and a professional storyteller. She holds a masters degree in education and taught elementary school for thirty years. She has worked as adjunct professor at The Citadel and Charleston Southern University in the field of education. She is on the approved artist roster of the South Carolina Arts Commission as storyteller.

Ms. Clary's first book of fiction, *A Sweet, Sweet Basket*, was published in 1995. It was very positively received and was listed among *Smithsonian* Magazine's "Notable Books for Children, 1995." Her freelance articles and children's stories have appeared in local and national publications. In 1990, she published a volume of poetry, *A Poem is a Memory*.

A South Carolina native, Ms. Clary has called the Charleston area home for more than thirty years. She and her husband Ralph live on James Island. They have two children and three grandchildren.

Ms. Clary is actively associated with a number of national and local professional groups including the National Association of Storytellers, The International Reading Association, Delta Kappa Gamma International, The Society of Children's Book Writers and Illustrators, and state and local arts councils.

About the Illustrator:

VALERIE JEANNE LUEDTKE has had no formal training in art and considers her natural talent a "gift from God." Ms. Luedtke is a native of Catskill, New York, but has lived in the Charleston area for twenty-four years. She is Director of Children's Ministry and Jr. Youth Leader at VineLife Church where she interweaves art into her teaching. This ministry, she says, is her real passion in life.

Ms. Luedtke lives just outside the city of Charleston with her husband Scott and daughter Rachael. Her work is exhibited locally.

This is her first book.